Way Far Away

ALSO BY EVELIO ROSERO
FROM NEW DIRECTIONS

The Armies

Good Offices

Stranger to the Moon

Toño the Infallible

EVELIO ROSERO

Way Far Away

translated from the Spanish
by Victor Meadowcroft
& Anne McLean

A NEW DIRECTIONS
PAPERBOOK ORIGINAL

Manufactured in the United States of America
First published as a New Directions Paperbook (NDP1591) in 2024
Design by Erik Rieselbach

Library of Congress Cataloging-in-Publication Data
Names: Rosero, Evelio, 1958– author. | McLean, Anne, 1962– translator. |
Meadowcroft, Victor, translator.
Title: Way far away / Evelio Rosero ;
translated by Anne McLean and Victor Meadowcroft.
Other titles: En el lejero. English
Description: First edition. |
New York, NY : New Directions Publishing Corporation, 2024.
Identifiers: LCCN 2023043033 | ISBN 9780811238076 (paperback ; acid-free paper) |
ISBN 9780811238083 (ebook)
Subjects: LCSH: Grandfathers—Fiction. | Granddaughters—Fiction. |
Missing children—Fiction. | Grandparent and child—Fiction. | LCGFT: Novels.
Classification: LCC PQ8180.28.07 E613 2024 | DDC 863/.64—dc23/eng/20231002
LC record available at https://lccn.loc.gov/2023043033

2 4 6 8 10 9 7 5 3 1

New Directions Books are published for James Laughlin
by New Directions Publishing Corporation
80 Eighth Avenue, New York 10011

for María Mercedes Carranza

Way Far Away

I

THE HOTEL LANDLADY TOLD HIM THIS WAS HIS ROOM: SHE opened the door and pointed to a cell, a sort of coffin. The stone bed looked like another coffin inside it. And on the wall there was a single, lopsided painting: the face of Jesus Christ, pale and bloodied, with one eye faded by the damp. Exactly like Christ winking at you.

He managed to wedge his pack in between the side of the bed and the wall, and prepared to go to sleep. With the cold night air seeping in, with the landlady observing him closely, it was impossible to think of undressing. He took off his shoes and slipped beneath the icy blankets. There was no pillow.

"You can use your pack as a pillow," said the landlady.

She was still there, inside the cell, as though spying on him. Illuminating her, in weak surges, was a bare bulb that dangled from the ceiling in the corridor, buffeted by the wind. If he fell asleep—he thought—that repugnant landlady would lurk over him for an eternity.

Repugnant because, aside from being the landlady, she also ran a raw chicken stall, located at the hotel entrance. While plucking one of her squalid birds—which she also reared and fed—slipping the chicken feathers into her bulging apron, chewing on a piece of raw cartilage, this same pale, plump landlady would also be showing you the rooms of the hotel. A hotel identical to the town. You are the only traveler at the hotel. And because after your journey you simply requested *the most affordable room*, the landlady has been left forever disappointed in you, leading you to the courtyard, then along an icy corridor and, with an expression of deep disdain, pointing to that cell with no air or light, almost a crypt.

"Thank you," he said, "I don't need a pillow."

The landlady was still there, in the doorway. Behind her, beneath the faint light from the bulb, the maid passed by, a bucket and mop in her hands. She stopped to peer in at him in bed.

"I think I should get some sleep," he said.

"And who's stopping you," replied the landlady. "You can rest easy, no one's going to rob you. And beware of the nightmares."

He was able to see how the maid—still only a girl, but with a face aged by exertion—poked her disproportionate head under the landlady's arm, and to hear that she was saying something, though he was unable to understand what she said. He only heard that they were both laughing, dissolving into terrifying cackles.

But he was already asleep.

He dreamed he wasn't in that town, in that hotel, that his search hadn't become so miserable he had to sleep there, in the middle of that cell, in that town, that hotel. Then he opened his eyes. He was still there, in the middle of the night, in the midst of that silence intensified by the wind. He was about to move, shift, and go back to dreaming, when he felt himself penned in, discovered that the landlady was also still there, standing in the shadow of the doorway, plucking another of her chickens, slicing through the cartilage with her teeth, the maid by her side. They were no longer talking or laughing, but continued to watch over him. Finally, he heard the voice of the maid:

"I think he's awake," she said.

"No," replied the landlady. "He's still dreaming that he isn't here in this hotel or this town, that he's far away from here."

And she sighed:

"This poor old man is in for a world of suffering when he opens his eyes."

"I thought I heard him open his eyes," insisted the maid. "I could hear his eyelids opening."

"You hear even what you don't."

The landlady advanced. He was able to make out her figure in the night, leaning forward. He could smell the raw flesh of the chicken that swung from her hands, next to his face. He immediately closed his eyes.

"He's asleep," said the landlady.

"And it's almost dawn," said the maid.

And they both withdrew noiselessly, and carefully closed the door.

Early the next morning, which was Saturday, the landlady requested he go to the store and purchase one or two traps for the mice. "They're everywhere," she yelled from the hotel doorway, as he made his way down the street, unwillingly attentive to his shoes, stepping on mist instead of ground. Mist and mice, he discovered, mouse carcasses scattered as though intentionally, blackened and desiccated, here and there, against a horizon that seemed made of plastic. It was dawn, and an icy cold came streaming down from the volcano. The street descended between puddles that resembled newly splintered mirrors; around their edges were rigid, congested carcasses of mice, their front legs as if pleading, seemingly still attempting to reach the water. The night before, when he'd arrived in the town, what he'd walked across like soft grass—sometimes hard scrub, sometimes crackling thorns—had been mice. No wonder the soles of his shoes crunched; it was the heads of the mice that he stepped on, crushing them without realizing it, the bones of their legs, their stiff tails.

Now, in the early morning, he at last discovered the infinite mound of fossilized mice, and on its horizon he saw himself, cropping up like a shadow sorry to find itself there, at the top of that unknown street, in that town strewn with mice, that town surrounded by the Andes, that town bounded on one side by the volcano and on the other by the abyss.

A bird could be heard beating its wings overhead, forcefully, for a few moments, only meters away from his face, and yet it was impossible to make it out: swift gray wisps of mist were sifting down over the town, separating it from the sky.

Scattered all along the street, at intervals, now-useless utensils poked up like the mouse carcasses in the mist. He saw perforated pewter cups and saucepans, shattered bottles of aguardiente, a headless plastic doll—its almost human skin standing out against the mist, the tiny open hands, as though switched on, appearing to scrabble in the mist; he saw a large wooden saint leaning against a wall, split down the middle and scorched from head to foot as if by lightning, a pair of flesh-colored women's underwear amid the sludge, and, unexpectedly, an old set of dentures with only three teeth, busted and mud-splattered but seemingly preparing to chomp. You look away from the teeth. Hanging from the grille of one of the windows lining the street is the head of a large dog, tied up with a leash. Strangled, its maw hangs open. A cloud of flies can be heard swarming around its head, inside its mouth, in its pointy ears. Again, the invisible beating returns, and swoops down beside you, at last detaching itself from the highest reaches of the mist, the enormous and indistinct figure of a condor coming to rest, a condor that's more white than black, its neck bare, its immense wings spread, then folded in, its reddened eyes alert, talons crushing stones, before approaching its prey with a hop and taking a vigorous peck, without ever neglecting your hurried footsteps beside it.

Yesterday he arrived at dusk. It was Friday. "If they ask, I'll say my name is Jeremías Andrade, I'm seventy years old ..."

He didn't want to feel that he was old, merely unwell: he carried the ache of the journey in the muscles of his neck, his knees, his heart. He became distracted by the view: it looked to him like a silent town, doused in water, with steep clay streets, closed-down businesses, famished dogs slinking around corners, washed-out houses, and that persistent drizzle of exasperating slivers of ice, which jabbed between his eyelashes like pins, forcing him to close his eyes. When night fell, he saw a dimly lit soccer field where a tall, scrawny kid scampered after the white head of a woman—a woman's head? The white head of an old lady—kicking it through puddles that appeared to explode with light. Plagued by doubt, he walked onto the field, an extension of the market square, and approached the kid, in the hope of a conversation, not just about the rolling head—why play with the head of an old lady?—but simply in the hope of conversation, to speak for the first time after all those silent hours of travel, and to speak to an inhabitant of the town, within the town, to hear the inhabitant's voice, as well as his own, to reassert himself on this journey, complete his arrival, bringing himself to life, although to live he would need to ask the kid if the thing he was kicking really was an old lady's head, and also why he was kicking the head of an old lady; he didn't get a chance to speak: as soon as he'd sidestepped him, the kid picked up the head and raced off, to the other side of that single light. He was left alone on the pitch. A night bird let out its hoarse, protracted song from the crown of a eucalyptus, and everywhere the drizzle renewed its percussion, as though in response.

So he walked to the square, opposite the church, still wondering whether that old lady's head had been one of those used at Carnival—sculpted from wood and cardboard—or if it was a genuine skull, a very recent skull, for it had been covered in white hair, the faded braids beating against the surface of the puddles. He was still alone, wandering around that disordered market square, between the pulled-down canvas awnings, the stalls with dismantled frames, and the bundles of trash. This was the only paved area of the town, filthy with peels and mice, with burlap and horsehair, with rusty cans and charred pilings; there were sections that were blackened and still dry, and others like small lagoons where, alongside the shiver of the drizzle, he believed he could make out the flickering of water as red as blood. Blood? Finally you went over to look, you even knelt, to better position yourself beneath the light from the only bulb, and stretched out your hand, submerging your index finger and then observing it closely, before you made up your mind and tasted it with your tongue, in the weak light from the lamppost, and yes, you discovered, it really was blood, surely from a cow that had been slaughtered in this very market square, the square used provisionally as a killing floor, or was it blood from the woman whose head the kid had been kicking? He was asking himself this very question when a new arrival leaned toward him, breathing into his ear for just an instant, the fleeting profile of a commiserating compadre, and said as if in response: "They carved one up just there, right where you're kneeling, that's where the realization of death set in." You stood up to look at his face, but the stranger had already leapt into the street, into the night, vanishing. All around were the damp stones, the as yet unsuspected mouse carcasses, the church, and the gray rectangular projection of bricks with little windows that was the convent of the Discalced Carmelites, where at that hour of the night—beneath the drizzle—singing could be heard.

II

THE TRUCK HAD DROPPED HIM AT THE ENTRANCE TO THE town, near the store.

The truck was now nothing but a trail of smoke on the main road that disappeared into the dusk.

Beside him, darkness was falling quickly in the corners, all straining toward the abyss: purple and blue clouds swirled and then furiously tore apart, distorting the atmosphere. The sun was plummeting. As its last rays faded, he had arrived in that town. Arrived at that line of houses aligned on the edge of the abyss. That town crisscrossed by streets that rose and fell like knives, that town of jagged triangles.

Dusk was still falling. In the chill of the first street he saw three men coming downhill, separately, distanced from each other, their bodies leaning backward as though in fear of tumbling into the abyss, their arms like pendulums, their necks craned so far forward it was as if they were presenting the backs of them before an invisible executioner, and he saw others going up that same street, but hunched forward, in complete submission, almost brushing the ground with their knees, in such a manner that when those coming down crossed paths with those going up, they resembled beings from different worlds, and they did not exchange greetings; it was as if each purported to be the only one, or wished to make clear to the others that they could carry on undisturbed, that nobody had witnessed anything, that they had never seen each other.

He unshouldered his pack at the edge of that corner, to rest.

None of those going up and coming down said hello: he greeted no one. He thought he glimpsed that they were young men, but they acted and walked like centenarians, their faces ruddy, their expressions contorted, as though marked by the intimate frustration of having to pass each other on the same street and pretend not to see each other and share in that mutual pretense—like a torment. It appeared to affront them. Like them, he preferred to ignore that they ignored him. He squinted and saw behind the men's blurry silhouettes, as though they were clinging to the final glimmers of light, the peaks of the mountains, and suddenly, like an icy, compact wonder, the volcano revealed itself, faded blue crystal, its peak lit up by snow; he saw it in its entirety and then not at all because it was immediately engulfed by a deluge of mist: in that single moment, the volcano had captivated him; then it became just another hazy triangular presence like the town, but a cross-armed colossus, an imposing threat.

On that corner, night closed in completely. He decided to go for a walk and ended up at the square—the kid kicking the head, the fleeting stranger. He left the square and returned to that first corner, to the curb, without meaning to. Now, dim bulbs illuminated stretches of each street. He sat there for a long while before another voice, but tender—"the voice of an old lady's head," he thought—a voice coming from who knows where and who knows why, told him there was a hotel in the town, as well as how to get there. "There's a hotel up there," it said. Its accent, like an echo, traveled along that street that dipped and rose and dipped and rose again like a straight line through the very center of the town, before arriving at the top and the hotel.

Now, on that leaden Saturday morning, en route to the store, a yellow door suddenly flew open, and an old woman simmering with rage emerged like an imprecation. Sinister, swift, armed with a bucket, she swung her arms and hurled filthy water at his feet. He had to jump back. Then he heard the slamming of the door and that steely silence, once again. In the black water that ran over the mouse carcasses, he saw distended chicken feet and heads, loose bones. Behind an open window the faces of two children appeared and disappeared, before appearing again, laughing loudly, and then disappearing, swallowed, laughter and all, by the mist.

When the children laughed, he slipped his hands inside his pockets, like some sort of instinctive defense mechanism: he wanted to smoke. He discovered he'd left his cigarettes in the room, and never had he wanted to smoke a cigarette so badly. A year ago, when he began his search, he'd started smoking again, and the children's laughter had triggered him, through pure shock. Their laughter froze him. "I should have worn an extra shirt," he thought. But he wasn't going to wait until he reached the store to smoke. He would go back to the hotel: it was closer.

He'd already had a cup of coffee for breakfast and was missing his cigarette. He'd drunk the coffee alone, in his cell, because the landlady and the maid had assumed he wouldn't be using the dining area, that he wouldn't cough up for a couple of fried eggs. What's more, he'd drunk his coffee cold. The landlady and the maid had served it to him cold inside his cell because, they claimed, "we figured you couldn't afford the breakfast, right?" and they'd stayed there with him the whole time, awaiting his protest, sulking, finally defeated, and concerned because he told them he would go for a walk around town, that he would go to the store. Then the landlady had followed him to the hotel entrance, and when he was already out on the street, in the mist, she called out her request for him to purchase one or two traps for the mice. "They're everywhere," she'd yelled, like an act of revenge. She'd hurled that warning like a curse.

He was returning to the hotel in search of cigarettes, climbing the steep street, and was able to make out its facade, which loomed up ahead, as merciless and inescapable as the volcano itself, oppressing him. The landlady was no longer in the doorway. The ancient facade appeared even more lonesome and abandoned, like the entrance to a cemetery. That's the impression he was left with, for the first time looking closely at the building in which he'd taken up residence the night before. The solitary, inevitable hotel. A mansion at the top of a hill that adjoined no other houses—only the steep street—and whose sole distinguishing feature was that tin sign above the wide entrance: HOTEL. And, underneath, on a crude placard, in small, unsteady letters: *Raw chikins fur sayl.*

The night before, it had seemed like nothing more than a building set back from the town, at the top of a steep street. Now, on this ruinous morning, it resembled a cemetery. He passed the grubby front desk, where the raw chickens dangled.

There was no need—he thought—for a fridge. The entire town was a fridge in which the body of every inhabitant emitted cold, induced it: this is what he'd felt with the landlady and the maid. This is also what he'd felt when the blurry silhouettes of the three who were descending and the three who were ascending had passed by him the night before on the corner, as if he didn't exist. Two of them had even brushed him with their ruanas, but hadn't said a word, merely left their trail of coldness and continued on their way. That same organic, tactile cold, which he'd felt from the old woman who hurled filthy water at his feet: he felt that she had also launched a breath of ice that had emerged not solely from her face but from her entire ancient body, straight at him, like yet more filthy water. But the laughter of the children had made him feel even colder—he thought—it was the laughter of the cold itself; it stung the heart, from pure cold.

It was this same cold that grew as he stepped through the hotel doorway, as he crossed the corridor toward the courtyard, where his cell was located, the last one on the ground floor, tucked on the far side of the old treeless courtyard. He wondered why the coldness increased inside the hotel. The hairs on his neck were standing on end, his feet were frozen, his heart numb. He found it difficult to walk. Through the fine ripples of mist, like the shimmers of an illusion, he could see someone's dark back inside his cell; he remembered he'd left his luggage on the bed. *It's the landlady*, he discovered, *she must be tidying the room*. He made a great effort to continue; he could see her arched back, wrapped in a black shawl, her calves in thick black socks, her gray galoshes, her plump arms, which were moving. The landlady wasn't tidying the room: she was rummaging through his pack. *What is there to find?* he thought. He stood motionless, behind the landlady. He could hear her cursing as she spread his clothes out on the bed and felt inside his socks, the pockets of his pants, his shirts; she found his underpants and began flinging them indignantly over her shoulder, one by one, while at the same time continuing to grope around; and then he saw the cigarette pack go flying, along with his clothes. The pack slid past his shoes. He picked it up and turned around. He would soon find a light, he thought. And he left the hotel for the second time.

III

"GOOD MORNING," HE HEARD HIMSELF SAY, NOT RECOGNIZ-
ing his own voice. And then he heard it again, in the mist, interrupting the advance of a burly fat man who was struggling up the
middle of the road: "Could I trouble you for a light?"

The mist thickened. It was as though night were falling in the
middle of the morning. The fat man wore an enormous woolen
hat with earflaps. His face was the beet red of an albino. His
blond eyelashes fluttered over small eyes that were like blue
streaks. The fat man was heading up to the hotel as he came
down, and was smoking, which is why he had waylaid him with
a greeting. He said: "Good morning," and the fat man responded
instantly: "There's nothing good about it," and then stood waiting, glancing in all directions, inspecting everything, except for
him. That's when he asked him for the light, and the fat man let
out a loud, fake laugh: "Trouble? Round here you can have all the
trouble you want." And the fat man held out his cigarette so he
could light his own.

All the trouble you want, he thought. He would have liked to set
fire to the troublesome wall of mice that surrounded them. He
looked down at the heap of mice, parting it slowly, carefully, with
the tip of his shoe, clearing himself an area in which to move
during the conversation, without having to tread on those mouse
heads—he thought—always sonorous, and for that very reason
scandalous, as though alive. If anyone were to approach, they
would be able to hear the crunching of mouse heads. Every step
would sound a warning.

He was busy trying to light his cigarette when the fat man huffed. He appeared to hunker down in the cold.

"So," he asked, "are you staying at the hotel?" With another glance over his shoulder, the fat man tried to ensure that nobody was snooping nearby. He couldn't see anybody, it was impossible to see a thing. Nevertheless, he didn't stop checking for other presences. Suddenly, his whole big red face, marked by the two streaks of blond eyelashes, turned toward him, intently curious. His voice changed: "Are you staying at the hotel?"

"Yes."

There was a silence. Another thick curtain of mist appeared to separate them eternally; only the burning tips of their cigarettes were visible. But a second later their faces reappeared, their eyes, their bodies, blurry through the faint drizzle they were beginning to hear on the puddles.

"Me too," said the fat man. He took back his cigarette and stood staring at the burning tip. He still wouldn't meet his gaze. "But last night I didn't sleep at the hotel," he said, "not last night or the night before. In fact, it's been months since I slept at that damned hotel. The landlady's a thief. Even though I haven't been sleeping at her place, that bloodsucker keeps charging me the daily rate, because I haven't officially checked out."

The fat man went silent again, as abruptly as he'd started talking. His face was sweating in the cold. Was he waiting to be asked a question?

"And you keep paying?"

Finally, the fat man looked him straight in the eyes, for an instant. His beady eyes were incredibly blue, the whites of the corneas bloodshot. He was staring at him furiously.

"Do you think I'm an idiot?" he asked.

Once again, the mist separated them eternally. Only the voice of the fat man could be heard, as though commiserating, sounding farther and farther away:

"I let her play her little game. She serves a good breakfast. I act as if I'm still her guest, and she acts as if I'll pay her someday."

Again, the mist was swept away by the wind, and both men reappeared.

He saw the fat man's black boot, the hard square tip stubbing out the cigarette, pressing it into the bloated belly of a mouse carcass.

"There are hundreds of these mice," he said.

"Mice," repeated the albino bitterly. "What mice?"

And he retrieved a bottle of aguardiente from his pocket. He took a long swig, without offering any, then put the bottle away and lit another cigarette: after a desperate drag, he looked at him for the second time, now without fury, but with malice glistening in his tiny pupils.

"And have you met the dwarf yet?"

"The dwarf?"

The fat man laughed, sincerely this time.

"Is the dwarf no longer there?" he asked.

"What, you mean she isn't a young girl?"

Again, he felt the furious eyes, deciphering him.

"What damned girl? She's a whore of a dwarf, and in more ways than one. Just lay out your merchandise and you'll see how she gobbles it down whole, balls and all and to the heart. You've got to have real stones to satisfy that one. She'll get through thirty in no time at all, but she's another reason I go there. After breakfast, bring on the dwarf. She's the only hole you'll find in this damned town; the rest are all nuns. Goodbye."

With that, the albino carried on up the hill, while he continued down. It wasn't long before the fat man called out to him, from the very top of the street, just as he was preparing to climb the next one.

"Old man," he cried. "You never told me your name. Let's meet again sometime, you can tell me why you came here. I've taken a liking to you. Around here, in this town, they call me Bonifacio!"

Behind the fat man's enormous hat, he glimpsed the hotel, its ghastly roof. The albino tossed his burning cigarette into the mist and didn't wait for a reply. He vanished.

"My name is Jeremías Andrade," he said, to nobody.

He remembered where to find the store, at the entrance to the town, at the other end, traveling downhill more often than up, descending like the cordillera, but he proceeded horizontally, taking the third corner, seeking out the side of the town that bordered the abyss. He stepped out into the mud. It wasn't so much a street as a narrow main road, bounded on one side by damp bushes—lining the abyss—and on the other, by a broken row of houses.

Above the peaks, the sky was actually visible; the mist was falling away. At the edge of the precipice, it seemed to him that the cold could even be glimpsed in the stones, that it was blue, like smoke, and floated in the enormous boulders in the distance, spreading like smoke all through the broken jungle, between the bright-white frailejones, weaving between the trees, leaping into the abyss. He became lost in the cold, its blue scarps, a deep precipice, solemn, like a cathedral. Much farther down, the narrow river cut like a shining ribbon beneath the mist.

When he looked back at the houses, on the other side, he found that they were all shut up, run-down, ramshackle, you might even say derelict.

The main road glistened with puddles, in stretches. You could hear the burbling of brooks. In the distance, a cart driver was coming toward him. Climbing slowly, as though in pain, the horse and the cart driver appeared motionless in the distance, almost like portraits; the cart driver was on foot, a pale, wide-brimmed hat partially obscuring his face. Inside the cart, a huge mysterious load was afflicting the horse. It must be carrying heavy bundles. Bundles of something, but definitely bundles, he thought, bundles from beginning to end. And the truth is that from time to time the driver did actually stop and squat down over the ground with his jet-black shovel and gather shovelfuls of something—smudges, dark stones—and deposit these into the back of the cart: they were mice, he discovered; the cart driver had set out early to clear the town of mice. There were so many, he thought, that there you were, trampling over mouse hearts with your shoes, amid the stench of their carcasses, and you were already starting to grow accustomed to it. One day you would grow so used to it that you wouldn't even notice them.

He had to start his search in that town; he had a single question that encompassed all others, but when would he begin? It was true he'd only arrived the night before, but it was time to start asking, or at least to start thinking about who he should ask. The landlady? The maid? The fat man who said that in this town they called him Bonifacio? The approaching cart driver?

He opted instead to slip around the corner, toward the heart of the town, the market square. At that moment, amid that stench of carcasses, he would have been unable to speak to the cart driver or anyone else, or even to get through half of the first question without interrupting himself to hurl out his stomach and his soul.

It must still have been early for the townsfolk; he now encountered no one in the streets. He was nearing the convent; coming from its cloisters he could hear the first Saturday hymn, very faint, transparent; the church stood out beyond it; blue smoke traced spirals behind the courtyards; a shock of birds rose up into the mist and disappeared, and then—devastating, contradicting the absence of inhabitants—he observed a nun in a white habit who had just cracked open the convent's broad metal door. On noticing him, the nun pushed the door shut again, with a bang, her face flushed, terrified. He looked around: he was the only person in the street, the only source of terror.

He continued walking. Now he could hear the chanting of the nuns more clearly. But he ceased to hear it when he reached the front of the church, where he discovered—strewn across the stone steps, before the closed church doors—the bodies of countless men who slept with their hats on, muffled up in their ruanas, open hands stretched out among the mouse carcasses, hands still reaching for empty bottles of aguardiente; they too appeared dead on account of their absolute stillness, their bare feet.

One of those defeated faces—slender as a knife, carved with wrinkles—sat up for an instant and spoke in his sleep, his voice a whisper: "It's best you turn back," he said.

This warning brought him to a standstill, as if waiting to hear more, as if waiting for the sleeping man to wake up and explain himself. He didn't wake; he said nothing more. And, as though this silence were a sign that the warning had nothing to do with him, that he was somehow exempt from fate, he continued on his way. He made a gesture with his hand, as though waving goodbye.

And he came out into the market square.

Now, as though stumbling, he came across a group of children in the middle of the square. They were circling something, some sort of mass, and occasionally prodding it with their feet, changing its position, laughing. It was that same dog's head he'd seen hanging from a window, the dog's skull, pecked down to the bone. He continued walking. So they'd detached it to bring to the square as a trophy. But who would think of hanging a dog's head from their window, he was asking himself, as he came to a halt before the children; there were six or seven of them, twelve years old and younger, and no sooner did they catch sight of him than they abandoned the dog's head, fleeing a short distance, without ever taking their eyes off him. They retreated to a street bordering the market square, lined with identical houses, all the same pale green. One of these houses stood out because of the sign on its door: HOSPITAL. This distracted him: the hospital was just like any other house. Inside one of its rooms, within the almost complete darkness of an open window, he thought he saw the yellow figure of a woman emerge, and that her saucer-eyed face was observing them. Her faded yellow mouth cracked open. He sensed her eyes watching him; watching him rather than the children. And since the children were continuing to retreat as he moved toward them, he stopped again. The children did likewise. Never in his entire life had he seen faces display such a mixture of hatred and fear. He was preparing to say something to them, to tell them something that might convince them he was made of the same flesh and blood as they were, when one of the younger ones, the smallest, wearing only one shoe—his other foot covered in mud— crouched down, picked up a stone, and threw it at him: it must have been due to the weight of the stone, and because the child lacked strength, that the projectile described a slow, gentle arc toward him. He had only to stretch out his hand and receive it in the center of his palm, as if the boy had thrown it for him to catch. Immediately, the children took off running, screaming, sure that he would throw the stone back at them.

They fled.

He stood there with the damp black stone in his hand, cold as a block of ice, and finally tossed it beside the dog's head. He carried on down the street, now resolved to go to the store, but then, from the open window of the hospital, from its yellowish gloom, he heard the woman summoning him.

"Mister," came her gravelly voice. "Mister," he heard again, more loudly, the graze of a hand beckoning him by force. "Come here."

The closer he got, the more he could feel the human ice that emanated from that woman, not only from her voice but also from every one of her pores, that woman who was again calling to him, pinpointing him within the mist, that ice appeared to now multiply with the half presence of that woman's body, leaning toward the window, her young but hardened features, her tangled hair, her two pupils like torches in the mist, just risen from bed, with large dark circles under her furious eyes, her voice lined with a fake tenderness, a sharpened curiosity. She was wearing a coarse yellow shirt, the bra straps coming down from her neck defeated by her ample bosom. "Mister," she repeated like a dagger, "would you mind telling me how old you are? You're not a little boy."

He continued to gaze at her in silence, taken aback. He wanted to understand what she was getting at, to anticipate her. It was no use. They could hear a bird singing. "My name is Jeremías Andrade," he began, but the woman instantly interrupted him: "And do you think it's acceptable for an old man like you to go around threatening children with stones?"

"I never threatened them," he said.

He wanted to explain himself, but the woman cut him off with a stifled cry, waving her open hands toward him.

"Do you think I didn't notice? Do you take me for a fool? Bonifacio's children were right there. I swear that if I tell him you were threatening his children with stones, Bonifacio will come and kill you with two shots right in your damn face."

And she slammed the window shut.

At the store he bought matches, a bag of bread rolls, half a dozen candles, and another pack of cigarettes. When he asked for mousetraps, the shopkeeper just stared back at him from behind the counter, as though waiting to see if he were joking.

The shopkeeper was a young but gray-haired man who wore large white-framed spectacles over his watery eyes, which were green and restless. A long black scarf was wrapped three times around his neck. In a corner of the store, sitting in a rocking chair, an old woman listened to them, dressed head to toe in mourning clothes. She was blind, but her eyes—half-open, like small wisps of cotton—seemed animated, seemed to flicker inquisitively in one direction and then another. Her hands were fastened around the handle of a cane, which she used to rock the chair.

"Traps?" asked the shopkeeper. "Did the folks at the hotel tell you I sold mousetraps? They were pulling your leg, mister," smiled the shopkeeper hesitantly, laying a big rosy hand on the countertop with the change from his purchases.

Now the blind woman's eyes seemed to peer deeply into other regions. Her piercing voice rang out:

"In this town mousetraps are no use."

The shopkeeper turned to her:

"Leave it, Mother, he's only just arrived."

"Here nothing works but poison," the blind woman continued, undaunted, "and that's why we don't have any cats, or have you heard one mewing? The cats died from eating the mice."

"I said leave it, this man isn't from our town."

"There are only mice, and we need to gather them all up and bury them before they bury us, don't you think? Those disgusting mice come from every corner of the globe to die here, this is the town of mice, the only town on Earth where all the world's mice come to die, the only one. Have you come here to die as well?"

"Mother," said the shopkeeper.

The old woman stopped rocking her chair. She tightened her grip on the cane between her knees.

"But haven't you tried the chicken at the hotel?" she asked. "Have you tried it? It tastes of mice, asshole, here the chicken breasts are fattened on mouse guts, or are you trying to make fools out of us? Do you think asking about mice is the best way to start the morning? Cocksucker. Go burn in hell, you son of a bitch. Or have you yet to step on a single damned mouse?"

"No one has stepped on a single mouse," said the shopkeeper, bizarrely. He gestured toward the change on top of the counter. It was three or four thousand-peso coins. These, he thought, were the last coins he had left, his last remaining money. But he said: "Keep it," and headed for the door.

"What?" he heard the blind woman cry. And he could sense her rise, as if she weren't actually blind, and scramble for the coins on the countertop. And then, behind him, he heard the clatter of coins against the wall.

"Your fucking coins are no good here," the blind woman bellowed.

IV

HE WAS RETURNING TO THE HOTEL. HE CARRIED THE BAG OF bread in one hand, the pack of candles in the other, and he walked back up the same street, later to descend again. The blind woman's fury continued to echo all around him, in the silence.

And then he was dazzled by the parting of the skies. The mist vanished, the last shreds swirling and dissolving in the corners, leaving the streets clean, transfigured by the light. It was a moment of sun, ephemeral, and for that very reason eternal, as it happened once a day. It was during that illuminated instant that he was able to see the shadows of the children reflected on the white wall of the street, the shadows walking beside him, faded, advancing in single file along the uneven shadow of the rooftops that lined the opposite side of the street, opposite the side of the abyss; then he turned to see them actually beside him walking on the rooftops, walking with him as he walked.

They were following him.

These were the same children from the market square, but on this occasion they were led by the tall, scrawny kid who had been kicking the old lady's head the night before. The children crouched down behind him, moving in a line across the rooftops; creeping last of all came the smallest one, peering down at him. As soon as they realized he'd discovered them, they disappeared. Nevertheless, very occasionally, as he walked, a head would pop out like a flash and look around. They vanished for good when the moment of sun disappeared. Once again, the shreds of mist took possession of the corners.

He crossed paths with a local, wrapped in a ruana, a scarf around his neck, with the indifference of stone, and another, completely silent, as though laughing secretly, and then still more dark neighbors, who emerged from their doorways without a greeting, without a word, those same pale hats, several walking sticks, their faces almost hidden, but in the end all their expressions were ones of shock, a concealed stupefaction on their countenances, no matter their age.

Back at the hotel, he realized for the first time that the courtyard adjoining his cell was a garbage dump. More specifically, a hotel garbage dump. How had he not noticed this earlier that morning? He saw the scattered fragments of porcelain sinks, toilet bowls, whole but cracked, some standing upright, others upside down, others lying on their sides, but all as if with real bodies sitting on top of them, as though the mere presence of the bowls, their chair-like form, could call forth the presence of a body. The same thing happened with the women's dressing tables: their dark oval mirrors insinuated the woman sat before them, gazing back into her own gaze. The same with the doors, all still possessing their frames, spread out like a deck of cards, leaning against the walls, other doors, or hanging in the air—many were suspended from a beam that ran across the courtyard—but actual open doors, their knockers primed, for their worn doorknobs betrayed the presence of gripping hands, different hands, they are doors that someone has just opened, he thought, that someone has just finished closing this very second, and you hear them. He thought about the only sound that was the same wherever you went: the sound of closing doors. Because all throughout this year of questioning he had heard them closing during his boundless search. On the uneven ground, of grass, of earth, of sand, there were rolled-up carpets, another headless doll, half a leather soccer ball, a soldier's boot, and, all of a sudden, an infinite pile of broken guitars, in a hazy white corner. He thought how impossible it would be to finish counting all of them that day, and then he thought of a guitar cemetery.

"It's not just the hotel that belongs to me," said the landlady, appearing from behind the pile of instruments. "All these guitars are mine as well."

She had done her hair in braids and was wearing a felt hat and her black shawl, and she walked through the hotel refuse like a fieldworker among her crops. She ascended the guitars as though climbing a staircase, stepping on strings that vibrated, snapping bodies and necks, crunching bridges and soundboards, every step sowing a furious music. Then she stopped, a cheerful expression on her face, hands on hips, atop all of the guitars.

"Yes sirree," she said. "These guitars are mine as well, I killed all of them myself, because my husband, may the Devil rest his soul, was a guitar maker. One way of getting back at him for his deceptions was to keep hold of all his guitars and smash them, because he's already dead, and I was left the sole owner, not just of the hotel and the guitars, but of all the chickens in this town, mister, the dead chickens and the living chickens, all those you can find in this hotel or at the convent, they're almost like my children, the chickens he could never eat. Why not? From stubbornness. His own guitar broke his heart, he preferred to spend time with his guitar instead of in bed with me, like any other man and wife, thief of my days, and let me tell you something, just listen to me: if there's one thing I won't stand for, it's people stealing from me, you hear? So I want to ask right here, with heaven as my witness, that you pay me at least one week in advance, or else you'll have to leave, because who knows what might happen, right? You could wake up dead from one day to the next, and then who's going to pay me? Pay me now so that we can both rest easy, that's what I've been wanting to say to you since last night, from the moment you arrived, but you looked so scared and tired that I preferred to watch you sleep, you had that same fear and tiredness you have today. What's wrong? Tell me. Do you want to sleep? You're too old to be wandering around. Why are you lighting that cigarette? You shouldn't smoke."

He stood staring at the burning cigarette. He was thinking about the dead man, the luthier, and felt genuinely moved, plunged into a pain he had never experienced before that moment. Because he too was an artisan, or at least he had been: a carpenter by birthright, since childhood, but more than that, a woodworker; he'd carved near life-size old men out of wood—old men that resembled him, wrinkled and sullen-browed after a journey on foot of almost a hundred years—old men who seemed on the verge of talking; hunched old men like him, which he sold, store to store, corner to corner, in order to survive. And because of that, because he knew and loved wood, he had reason to admire anyone capable of fashioning a guitar, which was akin to inventing sound, he thought, polishing it until you found its exact transparency, the necessary anima in the wood, and so he felt suddenly saddened, in the marrow of his finger bones, by that cemetery of ill-fated guitars, exposed to the elements, all that work and all that music, humiliated.

The landlady came down, treading heavily on the mound of guitars, and proceeded to the opposite corner, snaking through the jungle of doorframes, moving behind and in front of that swaying of opening and closing doors. Her hat appeared illuminated, alive. All of a sudden, he found her before him, as if she'd crossed the courtyard in a black flash through the center of the mist, a smile on her face.

"So?" she asked. "Were you able to find mousetraps?"

And she burst into laughter. Then she stopped abruptly:

"What? Did the blind woman get very angry? That one says she sees millions of mice. That's pushing it a little."

She waited expectantly, then shook her head:

"That one's like that. She sees millions because she's blind. And that bastard son of hers will die from rabies one of these days, those devils, they can both go to hell, they made their living by bringing us mousetraps, that's how they got started, selling us nothing but mousetraps; they arrived and the damned mice arrived with them, they brought a male and a female and set about breeding them, that soulless pair filled our town with mice."

She continued to laugh as she stepped into one of the hanging doorframes and went through, as if she really were passing to the other side, and yet, due to the mist, he was unable to witness her arrival on that other side. "I must be asleep," he thought, "my eyes are too tired to see."

"I'm going to sleep," he said then, and, as if in doubt—not about just this possibility, but also the other: waking—he thought: "And then I'll wake up." He was making his way back to his cell and, as if that moment of self-doubt had caused him to hesitate, stumbling, he said out loud: "I shall wake up," and afterward, suddenly exhausted but resolved: "Then I'll go up to the first person I see and ask them, no matter what time it is, and I won't stop searching, because this is the last place left to look."

He had been searching for over a year. Was he getting tired? He just stood still, hunched over, stiff from the cold.

"Then I won't ask anyone anything ever again."

On the opposite side of the courtyard, half-hidden behind the rubble, he could make out his cell.

The door was still ajar.

From inside, he heard a woman's laughter, it emerged sharpened with pleasure and rebelliousness, could be heard rippling like an arrow across the guitar cemetery. One guitar still had the strength to reverberate at the passing of that sharp laughter: it rattled with all its strings, a groan within the opaque luminescence of the mist.

The wind answered back, as he advanced.

There, sitting on the edge of the bed, under the winking Christ, as if having just readied themselves to greet you, flushed, submerged in a single bodily torpor—but always beneath the breath of the cold—their knees together—waited the man who said they called him Bonifacio in this town and the dwarf.

So she really was a dwarf.

He discovered her. She had the large head of a woman on the body of a ten-year-old girl, and her brazen face was smiling; she was like a horrible bird, for she reminded him of something horrible, but something as yet undiscerned, something unknown. The dwarf was laughing. She was wearing a schoolgirl's tiny checked skirt. Would she watch over him again all night, like the night before?

The albino continued to look him up and down. He'd taken off his hat. His hair seemed made of cotton, unreal, and was piled up over his bright-red forehead. His dogged attention contrasted with the pleasure in his voice:

"We were waiting here for you," he said. "Take a seat, old man, have a drink with us."

He suddenly embraced the dwarf, with gentle strength, his arm around her neck. From the hand of the embracing arm dangled half a bottle of aguardiente.

"Have a little swig yourself," said the dwarf, "or do you think it's too early? It's Saturday."

Again, she released that arrow of laughter across the courtyard, among the ruins. It was met by the death rattle of another guitar.

The dwarf ran her tongue over her lips. And then, without her noticing, the one they called Bonifacio began to tilt the bottle; the opening started to drip, trickling aguardiente into the dwarf's bra. She was wearing a white lace blouse. By the time she realized, it was too late. Bonifacio had sloshed aguardiente down the space between the buttons. The dwarf let out a cry of rage. Bonifacio was laughing. The dwarf shrugged his arm off. Her eyes flashed as she raised her arms, as quick as her cry, and she pounced at the laughing face, intending to pierce it with her nails, going straight for the eyes.

"You horrible pig!" she said, adopting another voice, husky, delirious.

But Bonifacio managed to escape her nails, with a shove, and was already far away from her. With a single bound he'd left the room, and, continuing to laugh, was running around and around the courtyard, sometimes disappearing behind the rubble, before reappearing in the most unexpected places, as if traveling through secret tunnels. He last appeared clambering to the summit of the guitars.

The dwarf went after him. She sprang into the courtyard as if flying. "You'll pay for that," she said. It now seemed that all her fury had become transfigured by happiness. She leapt after Bonifacio like a madwoman, laughing nonstop. Again, the guitars could be heard exploding. Finally, she cornered him, or he allowed himself to be cornered, and they began to roll around, embracing in the sea of guitars, without ceasing their laughter, as they stripped in the cold, kissing in the cold, becoming entangled in the cold, her on top of him, without the slightest concern for the cold, he thought.

V

HE SLEPT THROUGH THE REST OF SATURDAY.

And he woke at midnight, suffering from the physical sensation of a slow icy rain drifting from his eyes to his heart; it was the gaze of the landlady, he believed, hovering over his eyelids.

He floated in the darkness, as if covered by a single bedsheet, or as if that single sheet were pulling at him, raising him up; he thought he must be blanketless, that this was the reason for the cold, that he had uncovered himself in the night without realizing—this often happened to him—and that this was why the cold was colder; then he touched his chin with his fingertips, touched his eyelids, and believed he was not just naked but also rigid, frozen within his own coldness, actually dead, and he began to kick at the blankets until they spilled onto the floor.

And now, in order to revive, he convinced himself that he must be hungry, that his hunger had woken him. That must be it. He hadn't had a thing to eat in hours. This had begun happening to him ever since he started searching a year earlier; he would forget to eat; that must be it.

The darkness engulfed him.

Feeling around with his hands, he searched for the bag of bread by the side of the bed; the plastic had been torn to bits, and the rolls, soft when he'd bought them, now felt hard as stone. He groped along the wall, above the headboard, until he found the light switch; he pressed it; there was no light in his cell. He would have to go switch on the bulb in the corridor. "But I bought candles," he said aloud (more to hear his own voice, living, emerging alive from inside him, than to invoke the light). Beside the bread rolls, he found the candles and matches. The match's flame made him shudder: for a moment, the glare appeared to form a perfidious face—male or female?—which yelled something at him, as though spitting it. He lit a candle, and, on leaning down to stick it to the floor, was shocked to come face-to-face with an enormous rat, its damp smell, its paws fastened to one of the bread rolls; its phosphorescent little eyes observed him for a second; then the rat scurried away under the door, the sound of scratching claws splitting the darkness. He could no longer eat the bread; he couldn't get back to sleep either; he lay like that until dawn, and still the landlady's gaze remained stitched to his eyelids, forcibly showering him with cold.

He stepped out into the corridor. There was no one in the hotel. The landlady and maid weren't waiting for him by the side of the door, as they had on Saturday morning, with a cold cup of coffee on the earthen tray. He washed his face in the freezing laundry basin in a corner of the corridor; from there, he was again able to contemplate the wreckage in the courtyard: it had moved around during the night. A mountain of doors had replaced the guitar corner; now the guitars hung in a cluster against the far wall, dangling from rusty nails, as in an exhibition. Who had hitched them up, smashed to pieces, one by one? Like hanged corpses, he thought.

Only two doors were suspended from the beam, swaying and gently knocking into one another, as though someone had just passed through them. He decided to stop watching them dangle, for it was as though they were encouraging him to take a risk, challenging him to come forward and pass through them, to see what happened. The water ran down the back of his neck, making the hairs stand up. He drank a gourdful of icy water.

He stepped out into Sunday. At the main entrance to the hotel, seeking to take up his search again, he came across someone he hadn't expected: the cart driver, standing outside the hotel, leaning against his cart, with his legs crossed, darkened by his tattered clothing—blackened with muck—his pale hat, full of holes, a black cup of coffee in his hands.

He and the cart driver were alone on Earth, along with the horse that was eating freshly cut grass—a pile of soft grass that shone through the mist.

It was as if the cart driver had been waiting for him all this time, since the night before. Behind his black figure, the tall pile of mice was a dense, dark cloud; he saw how it spread across the sky, expanding, close to opening over your head, a heavy storm swamping your shoes, your knees, your breath.

And the time for asking had arrived, for resuming his search. He approached. The cart driver was a wrinkled, tough-skinned man, around his own age.

A man as old as he was, he thought, hard at work.

But suddenly, without so much as a greeting, he heard the cart driver's voice, which arrived as if continuing a long conversation:

"Like you, I'm not from around these parts," he said.

The cart driver took a long sip of coffee, continuing to stare into his eyes.

"That's why I do the work no one else will," he added, "gathering up mouse carcasses."

He tossed the empty cup into the cart; it landed upside down, on that mountain of mice.

"They've seen me so often they no longer see me, not me or the mice I gather up from under their shoes out of nothing but my own good will, because when the moment of truth arrives, the only thanks I get is a bit of food."

They were both looking around. There wasn't a single mouse

carcass in the vicinity. But they seemed to be beginning to sprout, springing up around the puddles. Spreading.

The cart driver nodded at them.

"I gather them up day and night. You might even think I'm fond of them, filthy carcasses, but listen, you can't get the stench of rotten mouse off your skin, and even when you swallow, it tastes of mouse."

And the cart driver became suddenly attentive; could he hear something? Could he hear some invisible being in the air who might be spying on them? He had dazed eyes, an aquiline nose, and his long white hair streamed down beneath the brim of his hat. He must have been able to hear something, because he added, in a whisper, as though ruling—abruptly—that some-one—one of them—had just committed a grave mistake:

"I'm like you, an outsider, and surely that's the reason I'm talking to you, on account of that coincidence. You can thank your lucky stars. If I were from these parts, I wouldn't even listen to you. Around here nobody talks to strangers. If somebody speaks to you, watch out. That's why I ask," and one of his hands grasped the shovel handle protruding from the cart, "why have you come here? How was it that you dared to come? You might never be able to leave, I swear it to you, with God as my witness."

He, too, like the cart driver, was looking around in all directions; he suddenly thought that it didn't feel like a Sunday. Had he heard the church bell toll? "I heard the tolling of the bell," he told himself. How long ago? A whole lifetime? Or had he simply imagined the bell tolling? The Sunday bell was tolling, the call to mass. It was Sunday. No wonder he hadn't seen anyone at the hotel. Apart from the cart driver standing before him, asking the questions he never wanted to hear, the rest of the town must all be at the church.

He took another step toward the cart driver. If they had stretched out their hands, they could have touched.

"I'm looking for my granddaughter," he said.

And he repeated the gesture repeated a hundred times during a year of questioning, his shoulders dropping, his head bowed:

"I'm looking for my son's daughter."

The cart driver did nothing, said nothing.

"Her name is Rosaura," he said. And from his shirt pocket, the pocket next to his heart, he took a photograph: he and his granddaughter laughing in the park. A blurry pigeon appeared to illuminate the bottom corner of the photo.

The cart driver leaned forward. His eyes remained dazed, inexpressive.

"A nine-year-old girl," he said.

He repeated what he always said, although this time he could hear the defeat in his own voice:

"In real life she's four years older than in this photo."

It didn't feel like a Sunday, he thought.

As if to refute this, the bell tolled again: the clanging cut through the mist, which was retreating as though inhaled by the mountains, sucked up by the mouths of the volcano. A patch of sun began to appear at the top of the street. The cart driver's voice seemed to arrive from that patch, illuminating everything.

"There's a chance you might find her," he heard him say, that's what he said, in complete contradiction to his previous words, his ominous warnings.

For the first time, he heard that hope.

They were walking down the street, between glistening puddles. The man had left his cart at the hotel and walked at a gentle pace, as though guiding him.

The cart driver was leading him to the church, and he allowed himself to be led, his hands clasping the photo as if it were the explanation of himself. Telling people that he was looking for his granddaughter, showing the photo, mentioning their ages—his own and his granddaughter's—but especially his own, ensuring that they saw he was old, that he'd be no good with a weapon, that he had no possessions, saying and repeating the same thing constantly, in other places, on other roads, even exaggerating his age and ailments—during that year of endless searching—had at least spared him from death. As a result of the sort of imminent death he embodied, countless weapons, belonging to one band or another, had been turned away from him, belittling him even in death. Looking at things this way, he thought, at least luck had remained with him so far.

They arrived on one side of the square.

"Now go and ask," said the cart driver, coming to a halt. Their eyes met. Then the cart driver continued downhill, while he carried on toward the church. There was nobody in the square, or on the field. The entire town must be praying inside the church. Those who weren't praying would be shut up inside their houses, he thought. The great doors of the church appeared before him. He understood that, in any case, he would have to wait until the end of mass. He could have stayed with the cart driver and talked a little longer. No. The cart driver had seemed to want to carry on alone. He would have to hear mass: he would hear it. How long since he'd last attended mass? "Rosaura," he thought, "help me to find you, wherever you are." Or did he prefer to remain outside, waiting for them all beneath that sort of fugitive shower of sunlight that illuminated the square, the field, the entire town. No. He would have to enter the church, like everybody else. He would ask them soon. "And I'll pray for you and for me, Rosaura, I'll pray for everyone."

He went in and stood in the final row, behind everyone's backs. The majority of those present were standing. You couldn't hear any priest's voice, only the voice of the church, multiplied by the loudspeakers: it was a silence comprised of the vast number of breaths contained in there, sonorous shadows that transpired, vapors of sweat from the bodies, small coughs transformed into otherworldly death rattles.

Again, the cold took hold of him. It was impossible to make out the altar: the tall heads prevented this, the damp shadow of the church. Had he perhaps arrived during the Elevation? Finally, he heard someone clearing their throat and a voice settled in the air—the voice of the priest?—a voice that sounded querulous and, at the same time, exasperated, a voice that sent its echo crashing into the towering adobe walls. Where had he heard that voice before?

"And now he comes to us," he heard it say. "He has just arrived and is among us, as if nothing had happened."

A number of those present turned toward him, their faces diluted by the incense. They were mostly women. He sensed the gaze of the landlady alighting on his eyelids, forcibly showering him with cold.

"Didn't I tell you?" Suddenly the landlady was very close to him, shoving her waxy face into his, and rebuking him, in the middle of mass, as though nobody could hear them, and yet everybody could: "I told you: '*This morning they'll remember you at mass,*' I said it very clearly, I said they'd remember you, and you appeared to be awake, appeared to hear me, sitting on your bed, but you must have been asleep. I gave you ample warning, and before I left, I said: '*You'll see, you'll see,*' I said it perfectly clearly."

The landlady's face vanished.

"Come down off your cloud," she said then, reappearing beside him, her eyes gleaming. "The last thief in this town was killed a long time ago."

Why was she saying this to him? She who, the day before, had been rummaging through his luggage?

He gathered, from people's coughing, their sighs, the almost delicate sound of chairs and benches sliding backward, the soft dragging of feet, the kind of anxious general impatience, that the service was over. Bodies pushed up against the landlady, who, in turn, pushed him toward the exit.

"Why did you say that to me?" he asked.

"Why did I say what?" the landlady snapped.

Now the bodies bundled them into a corner on one side of the entrance, beside the holy water font.

"Why did you come to mass?" the landlady repeated once more. "I warned you this morning, don't you remember?"

VI

PEOPLE BEGAN TO SPILL OUT INTO THE SQUARE. THEY COL-
lected in disparate, slow-moving groups around the small green
truck that had parked, who knows when, in the middle of the
soccer field. Two or three men were loading the truck with
chickens, strings of raw chickens, right up to the top. No one,
however, approached the vehicle, or its extraordinary cargo. The
majority kept silent. Were they still eavesdropping on him and
the landlady, on the conversation they'd been engaged in since
they came outside? Because, while appearing not to listen, from
time to time, someone would take a stealthy peek at them; these
were furtive faces, men's and women's, passing shadows.

The moment of sun was disappearing. Transfixed, he was paralyzed on the threshold of the church, and his gaze wandered
across the square, as though hastily drinking in the last sips of
that moment of sun—before the moment disappeared.

Sitting on a wooden crate in a corner of the square, between
large sacks of corn, barley, and potatoes, and bags of broad beans,
was the old blind woman, her cane resting across her knees; she
appeared to be watching him, her face turned toward him, pale,
round, possibly still furious. Her son stood behind her, one hand
on his mother's shoulder. What were they waiting for? On the
other side of the street, he was surprised to spot the cart driver,
leaning against the wall of the hospital house, his pale hat in his
hands, offering no greeting, no gesture; like the woman from the
hospital—who had again appeared at the window, though now
dressed in black—he too was busy watching without looking;

as was the dwarf, sitting behind a steaming pot, surrounded by clay bowls, a ladle in her hand, watching without looking, as was the entire town.

He turned back to the landlady, but she was already moving away from him, quickly and quietly, she, the oh-so-proud landlady, now almost as if she were afraid to find herself by his side, went slouching off to meet with the dwarf: she crossed the square without looking at anybody, hunched, ashamed, reaching the dwarf and sitting down beside her, behind the steaming clay pot, watching him without looking, like the whole town.

From behind him, he heard that imposing voice multiplied by the microphone, that voice coming from the very depths of the church.

As if the church itself were speaking, he thought. It was the voice of the fat man, he discovered, the voice of the albino, he continued to discover, the voice of the man who said that in this town they called him Bonifacio.

"This man, this newcomer," said the voice, "has revealed his name to no one since his arrival. It never occurred to him to introduce himself to anybody, to explain what he is doing here, why he's come, what he's looking for. He arrives and sleeps, then wakes up and goes back to sleep without introducing himself. And, if that weren't enough, during his first appearance in the street, he threatens our children with stones."

He could sense the questioning faces all around him.

Without realizing, he was slowly turning on the spot, as he looked back at everybody; his open mouth appeared to be on the verge of laughing—or screaming. Then he raised his hand and displayed the photo to everyone and no one.

"I never threatened any children," he said, as firmly as he could. And, nevertheless, his voice sounded feeble, broken, just like his body. The stupefaction made him tremble. And then he made the gravest mistake, he realized it himself as he was talking, *I shouldn't be saying this* he thought, but he did: "Ask the children." Then he thought, *the children will say yes, that I did throw stones at them*, so he immediately added: "I'm looking for my granddaughter, I'm just looking for my granddaughter. This is her in the photo."

He was looking into everybody's eyes; then he turned to the church, as though answering the voice of the building.

"She was seen in this town," he said.

The mist enveloped them once again, streaming down from the volcano; it came down over their heads in swift, white strips, shredded sheets. The moment of sun had now disappeared. But at least some hands were reaching out to him. Like slow-moving, indifferent blurs, the hands received the photo, returned it; his face and his granddaughter's face came and went like a ship floating on the hands; from a distance, he could make out the smudge of the pigeon in the corner of the picture, shining in spite of the mist. However, no face lit up. They merely leaned forward. The hands came toward him, retreated, returned, the photo always between different fingers, strong fingers, or pink ones, some like the fingers of a corpse, fleshless, trembling; their white fingertips, as though submerged in water for centuries, touched him, their faces watched him. Those same faces that had previously refused to even greet him.

In that vortex of bodies, he felt as if he were freezing.

"Look for her," they said.

Who had returned the photo to him?

And again, the silence and the mist separated him from everyone.

"Look for her in the losing place," a voice finally told him, from the other side of the mist.

"The losing place," he repeated, not comprehending.

And another:

"It's almost the same as the holding place."

"You might just find her there."

"The holding place?" he managed to ask.

"The faraway place," said another voice.

"Yes," they told him. "Go to the convent, it's the convent."

He peered into more faces. None offered any further explanation. Were they making fun of him?

And a voice:

"It's nearby, just around behind the church."

From somewhere, an incipient laugh made him shudder.

"I can find her there?" he managed to ask.

"Yes," they encouraged him, and the echo of that laughter did not fade—distant, secret yet present, its accents coming and going like a dagger. He'd heard that laugh before, too. Who? Where?

The albino, he thought.

But the albino was nowhere to be seen.

"You'll probably find her," they told him. "The worst journey is the one you never start."

He was heading to the convent, and, behind him, the town followed.

Or at least, that's how it felt, as if the entire town were trailing behind him.

He turned to look at the swell of faces. The cold emanating from those faces surrounded him, paralyzed him.

"Go on, go on," they told him. "Just keep going."

It was as if they were pushing him, without pushing him, he thought, like a lamb to the slaughter.

He felt himself besieged, held by the bodies beside him. So he stopped, and turned to look at them through the mist. He discovered that not everyone was following him. They had started breaking away in small groups, some already talking on corners, in whispers, others even making their way back to the square, lighting cigarettes, ignoring him forever. This sudden indifference encouraged him to resume his journey. Arriving at the entrance to the convent, he remembered that he'd already seen it open, on the previous morning. He thought of the terrified nun slamming the door with all her might.

And what if no one opened?

He looked for a way to call at the door, a knocker or a bell. He would have to settle for rapping with his fist.

"Wait there," they told him, "don't touch the door."

He wasn't sure who had spoken. Two or three groups were still with him; the rain started up again, the hats slouched forward, darkening the faces; the shadows began dispersing in the mist. He could barely hear their voices.

"Just stand there," they told him. "Sooner or later, they'll open up."

And another voice, sympathetic, but already hidden forever:

"They know you're here, that you've arrived."

"Yes," they told him. "Just wait to one side."

"That's the signal."

"Sooner or later, they'll let you look."

"Search carefully for her," they told him. "Do your best to find her."

The door to the convent remained shut.

He was still holding up the photo, but nobody was paying attention anymore.

The men disappeared. Their shadows passed through the curtains of mist, distant once more, like in the beginning. They'd asked him to tell them once and for all who he was, to give them his name; to some extent, they had demanded that he finish introducing himself, which was akin to asking him to tell his story, and yet now nobody, absolutely nobody, was paying attention.

"My name is Jeremías Andrade," he repeated to no one, "I'm seventy years old, and I'm looking for my granddaughter."

He stood there alone, for a long time. It was as though nothing had happened—he thought—or would happen. As though nothing was ever going to happen.

And then the door opened.

VII

THE SAME NUN WHO HAD SLAMMED THE DOOR SHUT, TERRI-
fied, the day before, now opened it, impassively, as though she
had been waiting for him. She had a rough complexion, and her
eyes, horrified when he'd first encountered them, did not look
up. Her mole-covered hand motioned for him to follow. He
walked behind her habit as though chasing white shimmers, for
the nun moved farther and farther away and then disappeared,
swallowed by a thicket of mist. A sudden gust of wind startled
them with hail, blanketing their heads like a wing, as they wandered around the front walls of the convent, the stone doorways,
one after the other, their arms extended, like blind people: the
back of the convent, he supposed, must therefore border the
abyss, face wholly onto it. How had he not noticed that side of
the convent when he looked into the abyss? It was yesterday, Saturday: he'd been dazzled by the river way down at the bottom,
the river illuminating its own banks with a green radiance.

The splinters of ice were turning them white. It was the wing,
hard with cold, that swerved above their necks, bearing down
on them. It seemed as if the volcano, hidden but nearby, instead
of spewing fire was beginning to spew more and more ice over
them. It was the wing, swift, fragmented, that continued to cover
them: beneath its white rain they wandered past the facade of
the building. Now they found themselves before a deep rectangular courtyard, shadowy like the convent, which adjoined
not only the convent building itself but also the town's longest
street. Only there did the wing—its piercing ice that reeked of

carrion—uncover them completely; they felt it depart between blasts of ice, as quickly as it had arrived, sparkling, moving off to the other side of the wall; and then they discovered the tremendous dimensions of that insatiable bird, the condor magnified. They saw it for a diaphanous moment, moving away from them, its fixed red eyes rising into the mist, alert, in search of its carcasses. Grateful, they watched it disappear. But the morning already seemed like evening: it wouldn't be long before nightfall.

He was searching in the strange light of the mist, as if this were the only way to finally find the answer, finally end his endless search. He was overwhelmed by that vista with no perspective, the grand old solemn courtyard, which contained—until they faded in the distance—a row of brass pots green with oxidation, refuse containers, one after another, equidistant tombstones, their dark round gullets crammed full of wet mice, whose black snouts floated like dark stains. It must have been from one of these containers that the condor, carved out of hail, had been eating when they arrived. This convent, he thought, was the cold's nest.

The mere presence of the mice reminded him of the cart driver, as did the sudden surprise of seeing the cart driver sitting on one of the containers, arms crossed, on top of his mice, unconcerned with gathering them up, just waiting on him and his search.

He guessed that the cart driver—as though following a sign—was looking toward the wall that bordered the main road, at the exact spot from which, moments before, the gust of the condor had leapt, setting off. He heard voices overhead.

There, balancing like cats—some standing, others seated—were the children, seven or nine of them, and they were bolstered by that tall, scrawny kid who had been kicking the old lady's head on the day of his arrival. It was their voices that now warned him:

"The losing place."

"You'll find her there."

"The holding place."

So they were still watching over him, he thought.

"In the faraway place," they said.

They hadn't stopped prowling around him. It was they, those same perched shadows on the rooftops whom he suspected of following him ever since he'd arrived in the town, those same shadows which he had perhaps confused with the entire town accompanying him. Now they warned him about the losing place, the holding place, they yelled down at him:

"Old man," they said.

"Don't forget."

"The faraway place."

He didn't see the white sheets in the courtyard, hanging in the wind, the black habits, pillowcases, and priestly garments, passing between them as if parting saloon doors; he saw only the wrinkled hand of the nun, pointing toward a great, shapeless hole in the side wall of the convent, as though made with the single blow of a sledgehammer.

Above it was a cross of laurel branches.

He simply peered in and called, "Rosaura?"

The nun's hand grasped him, urgently; her face and voice were full of pity: "Keep quiet," she warned him. "You'll have to search for her without talking."

The voices coming from the street, those hidden voices, started up again. They were no longer children's voices. They were the voices of women, on the other side of the wall. He was able to make out the dwarf's voice, the exasperated voice of the landlady. It was as if they were still talking to him by the side of his bed, he thought, spying on him, as he began to drift off. Or was he still asleep, for nights on end?

"That place is huge," he heard the women say.

"They scream in there. They scream a lot."

"If she's in there, no matter how close he gets, she'll never be able to hear him."

"They make an unbelievable racket. She'll have to spot him first."

"Because there's nothing in there but screams, he won't even know who to listen to."

"Go in and don't call out. Enter quietly."

"Don't let them discover you."

"Look for her in silence."

The rain was transfigured, beginning to swell like branches catching fire in the mist.

"Do nothing but look."

"May God protect you," the nun said now.

Far away, ever farther away, the women's voices could be heard:

"Let's hope he finds her," he recognized the dwarf's voice, straining against the rain.

"That place is enormous."

"It'll take him a whole century."

"He'll lose his life when he finds her," cried the landlady.

"What are they saying?" he managed to murmur to himself. And he searched, instinctively, for the nun. Why were they saying this to him? This wasn't hope.

In the roots of the mist, he continued to search for the nun, unable to distinguish her, until she turned, as if sensing he wished to look at her, and revealed her pure white face to him. "It's the mist," he thought, "it's because of the mist that I can't see her," for he could make out no eyes or mouth in that face, only a white, oval blur, radiating white flames. Finally, on the other side of the hole, he sensed the danger.

"This is what I get," said the nun bitterly, "for trying to play the savior."

"Rosaura," he asked again, leaning forward.

"Do not call to her," repeated a voice that was now excessively loud, monstrous, seeming to emerge not only from the nun's lips but from the very walls of the convent, from the rain itself. "Do not call out to one who cannot hear you. Go and look for her in silence."

It was actually the nun's hand, but he suffered it in his own flesh like a multitude of fingers—the rain itself—which propelled him from behind, through the hole in the wall. As if the hole were the exact size for his body.

Behind the opening, the darkness overwhelmed him.

He felt the cold intensify like another set of toes interlocking with his own: it wouldn't be long before they broke him down.

"Rosaura?" he whispered. But not a scream could be heard in there, not a single scream. There was only silence.

VIII

IT ONLY TOOK A MOMENT BEFORE HIS EYES WERE ABLE TO make out the fragile glow of candelabras, trailing off into the emptiness. In their paltry light he could discern the endless room, a sort of gigantic warehouse that must extend as far as the convent itself. The entire floor seemed to pulse and flutter, golden in the gloom: mesmerized, he noticed the multitude of chicks—still only small, newly hatched—which crowded together like a living carpet, beneath and around innumerable compact, rectangular shadows. Beds. He discovered that the place was seemingly sown with beds, all of them the same size: he counted seven beds wide by an infinite succession of them— made of stone, identical to his hotel bed—on which he could glimpse recumbent, reclining, defeated bodies that moaned and twisted above the almost invisible whisper of wings and chirping that swarmed underneath, in search of the warmth emitted by the bodies. For the first time he was disturbed by the smell, that mixture of farmyard and the throng of bodies. He took two steps forward, his shoes carefully parting the light and multitudinous barrier of pulsing chicks; there was a collective intake of breath: as a result of his voice, his presence, the bodies had begun to moan more, and even more as he advanced.

As if he had just woken them all up.

Then he called out, going against the advice of the women, he began calling out for Rosaura.

The moans erupted.

"Who called for Rosaura?" asked a voice, rising from all the other moans. "Who called for Rosaura?"

"I did," he managed to reply.

In that panorama of howling beds, in the yellowish light of the candelabras, his mouth hung open, stupefied.

He wanted to investigate the source of that voice, but it was impossible. Already, a confusion of voices around him—all crying out, asking him to come nearer—prevented him from identifying the voice, the body, the location of the voice, its bed. In his crushing desperation, he believed the voice had come from all of the beds.

"It was me," he yelled again. "I called for Rosaura."

"Would that be the Rosaura I know?" He strained to hear the reply among the voices. Now he believed the voice must be located in the bed closest to him, so he rushed over to it.

"She's my granddaughter," he said.

He couldn't even hear himself.

His hand went to his breast pocket and held up the photo. It was impossible to see the image in such darkness. He returned it to his pocket, hurriedly, as though fearing that somebody—taking advantage of the tempest of moans—might steal it. The voices continued to explode around him, colder than the blast from the condor, more merciless. It would no longer be possible to hear the voice's reply. Or perhaps nobody had spoken, perhaps there had been no voice? He could hear only the wailing—its warm rumble, its blaze-like din—now roaring; it deafened him; he felt as if he were sliding into a bottomless pit, falling through a circular swirl of screams, until the uproar forced him to cover his ears with his hands. In the faint light of the candles, he was able to establish that the person who had spoken to him—who he believed had spoken to him—lay chained to the base of his bed. And in that very instant, he believed it was himself who he found lying there chained to the bed, looking back at himself in terror as he and that other he in the bed pronounced exactly the same words at exactly the same time: *I called for Rosaura.*

He backed quickly toward the entrance, this time paying no attention to whether or not he trampled on the carpet of chicks that surrounded him; he felt them snap just like the mice in the infested streets, crunching beneath his shoes, except that the chicks were crushed alive; but that no longer mattered to him; he backed up; he found it impossible to tear his gaze from the immeasurable horizon of beds, the insufferable tumult of cries.

Outside, heavy rain replaced the sound of moaning.

"So?" he heard.

"What happened? Didn't we warn you?"

He was unable to recognize the women before him, each sitting in her own pew, arranged in a semicircle, and, he came to realize in his stupor, all under the downpour, all drenched in water, the same dark water that shook him like a blow. He was soon as drenched as they were, facing them, listening to them without understanding.

"We did tell you, didn't we?"

The water got in under his shirt collar, swamping him.

He saw that behind the semicircle of women the sheets were streaming, as were the habits, the pillowcases, everything hanging like stiff corpses. And, farther back, on the hazy horizon of the courtyard, he saw the cart driver, under the downpour: the pale hat, full of holes, offered no protection, yet there he remained, on top of his mice as if on a bed. Even farther back, on the far wall, he saw the white sphinxes of the children who watched on impassively, frozen to the bone, but livelier than ever. The mist was now being pulverized in the air; the downpour swallowed great mouthfuls of it, and the evening light illuminated the faces of each of the women beside him, each countenance bathed in rain, each expression—disconcertingly peaceful—under the fat droplets, which were luminous like wounds; the women's hair glistened, it stuck to their flaccid cheeks. They weren't bothered by the downpour; they simply persisted, their gazes hovering, waiting for his answer. But he just stared at them without understanding. In his memory, the chained voices continued to call out to him.

From among the women, from beneath the downpour, a nun seemed to emerge, startling him. Who was that nun really? He watched her advance slowly beneath the rain, another great droplet of water. She was carrying a copper pan in her hands.

Paralyzed, he heard her say: "You should eat."

And then:

"Do you want to eat?"

And she held out the pan:

"Eat something."

"Eat," repeated the other women. And then, because he remained motionless, as though hoping to convince him:

"It's *helado de paila.*"

He discovered that, beneath the downpour, the women were also eating large chunks of the ice cream, in pewter bowls. Neither the hotel landlady nor the dwarf was among them.

Again, the nun held out the pan to him, half-full, with a spoon inside it. He could tell it was a wooden spoon.

"Eat," the women encouraged him.

He began to eat.

"It will stave off the cold," the women told him. "Keep the rain out."

Now the nun was sighing.

"You'll have to sleep in there with them. Don't say I didn't warn you. Why did you call out?"

And a woman:

"Sleep? Maybe. But go inside and look for a bed."

The other voices chimed in, lethargically:

"An empty bed, of course. And then lie down and wait."

"Until first thing tomorrow morning, when the choir arrives, when the charitable nuns feed them, when their mouths are filled with soup. Only then will they stop screaming."

"And you'll be able to search in silence, face by face, and there won't be enough hours in the day. There are hundreds of them."

"Hundreds," he repeated.

"Tonight, there's no option but to wait."

"Tonight, they'll howl."

"They'll erupt when they remember where they are, and they won't be able to sleep, because you've woken them, poor wretch. How could you even think of throwing stones at those children?"

"Stones at children?" he recalled.

"You won't be able to sleep either," a harsh voice interrupted him. And, finally, he discovered the blind woman. How had he not recognized her? With the cane in her restless hands, and still bearing something like hatred in her lifeless gaze, the blind woman allowed herself to become soaked beneath the downpour, her face turned up to the water, content.

"You won't find anybody," she said, revealing her long blackened teeth.

And again, the downpour retreated, savaged by the wind; waves of murky water were severed by the wind and swept far away, into the abyss. From the living darkness of the hole, the wailing became clearer (like yet more bubbling water), but the words of the blind woman also increased in volume, until they were all he could hear:

"And if you aren't going to find anybody, then why hurry? You'll end up in chains like the rest of them, you'll be just one more body, one more screaming scream, and no one will come looking for you because no one will find you. You'd do better to get out of here, if you can, because I doubt you can anymore, it's too late for you."

"Now goodbye," said one of the women, rising to her feet: "Someone here is running late."

At that, the others sighed and shook their heads. A thin vapor encircled their hair, like halos. They departed calmly, surrounding the blind woman. After tossing the empty pewter bowls into the pan, the nun followed them. Every so often the women would stop, turning their faces up to the sky as if demanding more water.

The screams and wailing continued to babble from the dark hole. He wondered if it would be possible to remain inside there for the rest of the night, submerged in screams.

"Find a bed," came the cart driver's voice, from behind the hanging sheets.

He was unable to tear himself away from the screams expelled by the hole, to one side of the semicircle of empty seats.

But again, he heard the cart driver's voice:

"Come and sit over here," he invited him.

The cart driver was sitting in the same place, lighting a cigarette. They smoked together. Only once they'd put out their cigarettes did the cart driver speak again:

"If I were you, I'd go through and find a bed, as you were advised to," and he crouched down on the ground and started separating out a group of mice, piling them into pyramids. "Look," he said, "despite appearances, all of us here are in the care of those bedbound folks," his eyes indicated toward the hole. Then he began to laugh, furtively; the cart driver looked like someone else, a stranger, perhaps even an enemy, he thought. He saw that the cart driver was rising to his feet. His voice was different when he next spoke: "In this town, nobody tells it like it is," he said, "you understand?" The cart driver held out another cigarette and, because he didn't take it, pressed it into the palm of his hand. "Go and smoke," he told him. "Wait till dawn. You'll be safer in there than you are out here."

And, before leaving him, he asked again, as if in condolence:

"But who told you to go provoking the children of this town?"

IX

HE HAD FINALLY COLLAPSED ON THE OTHER SIDE OF THE hole, in that smell of farmyard, his back against the wall, facing the multitude of vanishing beds and bodies and the living carpet of milling chicks, and it was right there that he immediately fell asleep, his hands pressed together as if in prayer, and yet still he doubted, in his sleep: it could all be a mistake—he dreamed—this was bound to happen to me too one day. When he awoke, consumed by panic, he did his best to remember. He couldn't recall a thing. Petrified, he attempted to get to his feet. It was useless. *I'm looking for Rosaura*, he finally remembered. He was going to find his granddaughter Rosaura, and it would be once and for all: never again would he send her to buy roses from the store, so that she would never again disappear; because she had vanished while buying roses: never before had he sent her to buy roses from the store, only bread and sugarloaf, but that time they had gone together to the store and seen how, on top of sacks of rice, like a miracle, they were offering that large bunch of roses that made his granddaughter cry out with joy. Neither of them considered the possibility of purchasing such a bunch of roses. They paid for the bread and sugar and left the store, shrouded in a premonitory silence, for they had reached the live-in workshop—the house he rented in an old artisanal neighborhood, the house where only he and his granddaughter now lived, since his son, and his wife also, had been killed by the war—when he put his hand into his pocket and felt that he had the exact six thousand-peso coins required to buy the box of iron nails he needed, and nevertheless he said to Rosaura: "Go get those roses, before I change my mind," and she had raced off to the store and vanished. She never came back. For a bunch of roses, he thought. Now he was looking for Rosaura. He would find her. And after he'd found her, they would escape—he couldn't imagine how, but they would escape—because he wasn't carrying a single coin in his pocket with which to pay what they would demand, not one simple round coin, he had nothing, unless you counted himself and his life, because he didn't own a thing, just his life, that's it, he thought.

"Rosaura," he said again, hopelessly. *It's Rosaura*, he discovered. But the young girl, who had at that moment been watching him from her bed, her eyes shining from behind her chains, stopped looking at him and went back to sleep. "Rosaura," he called, and his hands beckoned to her. Once again, he was assailed by weakness. He would have to drag himself if he wished to reach her, and nobody could help him, nobody helped anybody, he was as alone as everyone else inside that warehouse full of more and more chained people, all cold, dark, resigned. It was as if no one else existed, only him and that inevitable horizon of abject beings. In the heart of that moment, he believed the girl parted her lips and responded, or tried to respond. "Rosaura," he said, but her eyes remained closed, and he gave up. On the brink of defeat, he tried to hear Rosaura's voice in the current of bodies. His mouth opened as though with laughter: all these years, he thought, Rosaura had been the only thing separating him from death.

And he froze in the midst of those other souls lying before him. He would have to drag himself in order to examine them, one by one, until he found Rosaura. He was assaulted by a multitudinous din. Were they screaming?

Hopelessly, he went back to questioning the girl with closed eyes. Her lips were moving. Was it Rosaura? Uncertainty asphyxiated him as he managed to turn his head, now looking for the sky: he found only mountains of chained up bodies. It was as though a sky of blood were crushing them all. He shook his head; was he dreaming? He had been dreaming, but the beds in the distance and the multitude of frozen bodies reestablished a more terrible and concrete unreality, that is, reality itself.

He stood up, his legs numb, his arms paralyzed. He observed the recumbent bodies, the lost gazes, gone, the wrinkled faces of forcibly aged men and women, all of their hands fastened to chains that linked and sank into the yellow chirping of the chicks, the living carpet of feathers that trembled restlessly, pecking at kernels, flapping like a single desperate being.

The chained people were also feeding themselves, slurping spoonfuls from the soup plates that columns of nuns were setting on their chests. How many hours had he been asleep?

On the horizon, he glimpsed the figures of the hotel landlady and the dwarf, two hunched shadows, each with a sack over her shoulder. They were busy selecting the biggest and plumpest from among the chicks; they checked under the beds, trapped them, and tossed them into the sacks, and then carried on, slow, indifferent, concentrated.

Were there really so many nuns on the horizon? Innumerable, they stood out at every turn, with no priest to preside over them. He had gone the whole night without hearing a single scream, and woke beneath the morning light that breached the contours of the hole, the pale blue light re-creating the shape of the hole, as if all the morning—the entire morning—could be reduced to that, the hole, its formless dimensions; blue, but a minuscule blue.

Columns of nuns were serving the soup—in the aisles separating the beds—while another vast, white rank positioned itself around the edge, hugging the infinite perimeter of the walls, where the yellowish succession of burning candelabras—stretching like a merciful beam from the opening—bathed them in a dubious, otherworldly light.

And now they began to sing. He couldn't really hear them, just saw the chanting in their moving lips, raised eyes, joined hands. These must be the same songs of praise he had suffered through on Saturday morning when he passed by the convent. The nuns sang in white while the ones in chains slurped the beet soup, red as blood.

He too was approached by one of the nuns. He too was touched by that strange mercy. Because in the midst of so many deathly white faces, he thought, it was a strange mercy to offer food. The white mercy that moved over the living carpet of chicks, the floating nun before him. From her, he received his plate of soup, like all the rest; he sat back down on one side of the hole and, like all the rest, began to slurp spoonfuls, dumbstruck by hunger.

X

"THE LOSING PLACE IS THAT DOOR AT THE END, MISTER."

The dwarf was by his side:

"Can you see it? Way over there, on the other side of all these beds."

The dwarf's sack was crammed full already, thrown over her shoulder. Her gaze drifted, illustrating the depth: it was infinite, and yet, unreachable on the far side, there was a very narrow light.

The dwarf continued to talk in a low, urgent voice.

"This place here, where you and I are standing, is the holding place. The losing place is that door at the end, mister, the faraway place itself, if you like, that eternally open door, no matter the weather, a door to the abyss, go look through it and you'll see."

The dwarf didn't wait for his response; she stepped through the hole without saying goodbye. Behind her went the landlady, her pride hunched under the weight of her sack. She didn't so much as greet him. The humbled landlady. So—he thought—this was the woman who'd watched over him as he slept?

Humbled? he asked himself. Not a bit. The landlady turned to face him through the hole, as if taking her revenge:

"But let me warn you," she said. "For each of these bed-bound folks a sum of money is demanded. If nobody pays, then there they stay, till kingdom come. And if they pay too quickly, the price is doubled, to see what happens. Sometimes they bring double, sometimes they don't. And if they're too quick with double the amount, it becomes triple, that's just common sense. I warn you again: here everyone must pay; no one can escape that, especially not you."

He couldn't tell whether that warning wasn't also a wish. In any case, the landlady's head disappeared.

He set the half-empty soup plate down on the ground and stood up: a voracious vortex of chicks surrounded the plate at his feet; the birds drank the red soup, thirstily; they raised and lowered their beaks giddily, as if giving thanks to the heavens. The chanting persisted—just like soft chimes. He came to a decision and began advancing along the central aisle, now feeling as if he were inside a church, but a church erected on terror, because already the wailing was flaring up sporadically, in places as close as they were distant, wailing that was quiet yet piercing, wailing that threatened to turn into a roar, allowing itself to be heard like a shocking counterpoint, overpowering the very chanting of the nuns, wailing that paralyzed him once and for all before the first face he saw: a woman in her death throes.

"It doesn't matter," he repeated, "Rosaura will recognize me, she'll call me by my name."

He made another attempt with a different body, a different face. He leaned forward, and they both stared at each other. He felt he must be going mad: he felt as much like laughing as he did like crying, both at once.

"I must be unwell," he thought.

He decided to walk without looking. Rosaura would recognize him, he thought. He couldn't tell how long he spent advancing between the bodies, like a long, hard trek, either because he was old and sick or because his feet were feeling the effects of an arduous journey, a year of asking. He regretted not having finished the soup; once again, hunger debilitated him.

A sudden stench of viscera made him stop and stumble, to the point of nausea, a furious odor that cut through the air and pierced his lungs like a knife. All the beet soup rose up into his throat. He steadied himself as best as he could. A drop in temperature left him trembling; he leaned against one of the beds for support: the body occupying it felt stiff, rigid; all of the bodies in that place appeared dead; there, the warehouse opened out; the floor was damp, slippery, and it sloped noticeably downward: there wasn't a single chicken scratching within its filth; with nothing but candlelight—not a sliver of daybreak shone there, the hole had been left far behind—he made out a bunch of bodies lined up against the wall, squatting, almost naked, their hands supporting and distributing their own chains around them, defecating over a kind of drain that ran along the bottom of the wall, like a stream; the water could be heard running down the slope of the building, toward the inaccessible light, the losing place.

There were no nuns singing in that area; their hymns were left behind; only the nuns distributing soup wandered there, swift, mercurial, carrying on their work. And then the choir's chants vanished. They too seemed to have been forever chased off by the purulence, separated from the beds and the bodies, as if by some kind of wall. He snaked his way through the stench, and for the first time became afraid of collapsing, of fainting from nausea, from shock, from old age. He sensed that the faces in the beds were now beginning to assess him, *him*. Now they would begin calling to him, and all of the hands would be extended. He ran toward the light, ran until his faltering heart immobilized him. Would he have to drag himself along, as he had in his dream, in order to make it? Slowly, hands outstretched, he pressed on. As he neared the losing place, the darkness became lit by morning light; but he didn't turn back to look at any more faces: he could tell only that they were watching him, and that there might be other faces, different from his, or—sooner or later—his own face looking back at him.

He advanced with the patience of one embarked upon a long journey. Hadn't the dwarf told him that this was the faraway place itself? And there, in fact, was the door, in the distance. He could finally make it out. He was surprised: it really was a large door after all, wide open. Long before he reached its threshold, when he was just starting out, it had resembled nothing but a rectangular piece of sky, as if instead of a door it was a tiny window, a scar in the wall. Now he discovered the true dimensions of the door, like the entrance to a gigantic stable; even the threshold resembled some kind of terrace, about six or seven meters wide by eight meters deep, with no railing, like a viewing platform; now he understood why they called this the entrance to the abyss, the losing place. For a coldness from outside came toward him and overwhelmed him. It prickled like invisible ice on the back his neck. At least the pure air helped him to recover from the stench. He took great gulps of the cold. There, the dawn light had turned white already, and it dazzled him as he crossed the terrace and looked out. The impact of the icy wind made him bristle; the horizon opened out; from there, the precipice plunged downward: the mountain descended steeply. Beneath his feet, he felt the landscape spin like vertigo, a tumbling of the sky and earth together, through spirals of mist.

He looked down and could see the poor outline of his shoes presenting themselves to the immensity.

And he discovered the watery-green, almost chalky-white trail that descended—from his feet, at the edge of the terrace—to the distant riverbed, a downward path, a slick that vanished into that chasm lined with rocks and bushes.

Not too far away, the water from the drain spilled out, the stream of filth flowing sinuously.

Now he became terrified: some had told him that his granddaughter could be found in the holding place, others in the losing place.

Most had said that she was in the losing place, he thought. Or was it the faraway place?

"In the faraway place, way far away," he was repeating to himself, when he sensed someone beside him. It was that same nun who had brought him here, the nun who had led him to the opening, through the rainstorm. Her face appeared much older, her hands were clasped, and her eyes looked reluctantly into the abyss, at the downward path, filled with pure horror, as if she had finally dared to look only because he too looked down, because he was there, by her side.

"It's a painful path," she said.

Her lips were trembling:

"A path carved by the bodies that fell and fall, by those that continue to fall and those that will fall, the path down which they toss the chained dead, the most gravely sick, the chains still binding them, so that the river, below, can receive them, and its fast-flowing waters swallow them."

He saw her recoil, her expression contorted.

"May God protect us," he heard her say, crossing herself, her eyes immersed in the emptiness. "It's farther down than I imagined."

A puff of wind inflated her habit; she resembled a bird preparing for flight, albeit involuntarily. Her mouth moved, wordlessly. Then each word rang out, tinged with fear:

"There, where you're looking, over the precipice—how could you have dared to look?"

Her eyes tipped back, awestruck.

"That's where Mother Beatriz and Sister Brigitte jumped only last week. They couldn't take this anymore, dear God."

She brought her hands to her temples. She was looking to the heavens.

"Like me," she said.

Suddenly, she looked down into the abyss and cried out:

"My Lord God, the strength and warmth of our hearts."

In vain, he reached out his hands.

The scream was like that body in the mist, tumbling toward the river.

XI

"AY, AY, AY. ANOTHER FALLEN NUN."

He didn't recognize him, to begin with. The man was wearing a panama hat rather than the woolen one with earflaps; he looked different, perhaps fatter, his eyebrows less pale, his face less rosy, and he was armed: the butt of a revolver bulged at his waist. In the midst of the cold, the albino was sweating. He took the bottle of aguardiente from his pocket and looked down into the abyss as he drank.

"They should be grateful," he said.

He took a long swig and tossed the bottle into the abyss:

"But they get stubborn."

He continued to peer down into the abyss, as if speaking in whispers to the nun who had jumped, as if the nun could hear him.

"They want us to serve them, as well."

And he yelled, softly:

"Damn it, can't they just be content with what they have?"

He raised his eyes to the sky, toward its great leaden dome.

"Caring for the chained, instead of getting chained up themselves, is a miracle from heaven."

And the albino turned to him, arms wide open, a smile across his broad face, which glistened with saliva, his voice thunderous and drunk:

"What's up, old man, don't you remember me? Around here they call me Bonifacio."

From the depths of the holding place, a group of nuns approached the threshold of the large door—that sort of terrace—where the profiles of the two men stood out against the mist. Timidly, as if asking permission, their mouths and hands open, silent but as though screaming, the nuns also wished to look down into the abyss, or were intending to do so. They were a tight-packed herd; occasionally the wind would lift their habits, briefly, making them balloon and ripple sonorously, sonorously. The albino startled them with mock applause.

"Back to work, sisters," he said. "Oh blessed little *madrecitas*, we're going to have to lock you up as well."

The nuns fled in terror at his clap; a number of them screamed as they ran back across the terrace and crouched behind the nearest beds, mindful of the people in chains. Suddenly, the voice of one of the chained could be heard, hoarse, broken: "What are you up to now?" Many of the nuns appeared to be weeping in silence. Ringing out, as if in response, came the sporadic wailing, the dragging of chains in the depths of the holding place.

"I like you," continued the albino. He was scratching his head under his hat, as if he'd just remembered something very important, definitive. "I like you," he repeated. And he put his hands on his hips and shook his head, as though sorry to have remembered that very thing: "I *do* like you," he said.

The wailing interrupted him for another instant; then it quieted down, disappeared, swept away by a gust of wind. They thought they heard the wailing also leap into the abyss, vanish, absorbed.

"And if I like you so much, it must be because you're going to have to tell me who allowed you to reach this faraway place," said the albino, and he glanced at him for a moment, suspiciously.

Then he looked slyly toward the holding place, at the nearest nuns, half-submerged in the gloom, still shocked. It was as if he'd never even noticed the presence of those nuns. "Who brought you," he said, biting off each word. "Why did you accept help without consulting me? That's like an insult to the person who first greeted you, who gave you a light. You know, I'm curious to find out who dared bring you here. Who in this town dared?"

He was thinking of the nun who'd thrown herself into the abyss: it was she who had led him to the faraway place, through the rainstorm. Or had it been the cart driver? And he said only:

"I'm looking for my granddaughter."

"We know that already," replied the albino. And he smiled: "What I'm asking is who brought you to this faraway place."

"Everyone."

"Everyone?"

The albino's eyes bore down on him. The silence seemed to bring the two men closer together, into each other's confidence.

"Question by question, I arrived here."

"Really?" the albino countered. "Like one leap at a time."

"I showed them the photo. Someone said I might be able to find her here."

"Someone?"

"Someone."

"I like you," said the albino. "You're kind of deaf, and that's why you have trouble understanding us. Come, walk with me."

The albino put his arm around his shoulders, and they walked along the edge of the abyss; you might have thought they were about to plunge over, still embracing. But the albino stopped, stopped him, at the extreme right edge of the terrace, at the far end of the convent building, and pointed toward this final side: a projection of the brick edifice that stuck out like a round nose over the immensity. Beyond it lay the other edge of the abyss, and the main road—the strip of town that bordered the abyss. The albino continued to point insistently toward that side of the convent. And now he turned to him:

"That's my other way of getting back," he said, "without having to go past all those spoiled so-and-sos." His mouth signaled crudely toward the holding place; then he again pointed toward that brick nose, the height of seven men, which appeared to float in the emptiness. A brick ledge ran along the bottom. This is what the albino's mouth was now pointing toward: "You just have to climb onto the ledge, preferably without looking down, right? You simply walk across that ledge like a river, it's only twenty steps, I've counted, it's not the first time I've served as a guide."

He smiled:

"And, at the end, we clamber up that headland, you see? We reach it, go over the top, and then we dance for joy. You go first, I'll follow."

He didn't move.

"Go on, go on."

The fat man's arm pulled him even closer to the corner leading to the brick projection. The tip of that nose must surely sit above the convent's kitchen, because it resembled the ruin of a gigantic clay oven suspended over the abyss; its curved wall, slick with rainwater, slimy, pointed toward the drain. The ledge was made of brick, it was the exact width of a single brick; this cornice ran along that final stretch of the convent just like a long wrinkle near the bottom of the nose, formed of bricks that were damp, icy, and green.

The hand pushed him gently up against the nose. The hand was warm; the fat man was boiling.

There was another faint wail from the chained ones, as if it were striving to climb back up from the abyss. Then they heard how the wind swept away from them, swirling far from the terrace, sinking to the bottom like a great sigh. They could hear it down below, drifting above the river.

"Go on, go on."

He readied himself: was there any other option? The albino stared at him in fascination. And, as he raised his knee and planted his shoe on the ledge, his face against the bricks, and then landed his other shoe, right up against the wall, and began to advance, one step, two, his arms stretched out on either side—at head height—his fingers wedged into the gaps between the bricks, a strange insect half-crouched over the abyss, a rigid trembling, the albino whispered:

"You should have stayed at the church when you heard me say what I did, I was talking about you. Who else could I have been talking about, old man?"

"I didn't throw stones at those children," he replied, and he paused. His head turned to look back at the holding place for the last time. His eyes returned to the distant doorway, piercing the shadows as if desperately seeking assistance from the nuns, from the chained themselves.

"I want to find my granddaughter," he said.

"The last time I saw her," replied the albino, "she was breast-feeding a small child. Imagine that, you might already be a great-grandfather."

And the albino leapt joyfully onto the brick ledge, also facing the brickwork, then caught up with him and, with one hand, patted him on the head twice, three times:

"Go on, go on," he told him. "We don't have all day."

Many of the nuns had now returned to the terrace, to peer into the abyss, and were examining the path of the bodies and the river, searching in vain for the last body to disappear, the body of another nun, and then they looked at the two men, ended up looking only at them, in stupefied silence, pointing toward them, crossing themselves.

One of the nuns began to pray.

"Hush now, hush now," came the voice of the albino. He was smiling. He moved forward, forcing him to move forward as well—in the panicked silence, above the gray hollow of the horizon.

He shuffled along, one knee after the other, with the slowness of centuries, each kneecap pressing into the wall: he could feel his own heart pounding. His terrified hooked fingers earned a guffaw from the albino, who shook, trembled, and slapped a celebratory hand against the wall. Suddenly, the straw hat brushed against the brickwork, tilted sideways onto the albino's forehead, slid across his sweaty neck, and swooped down into the abyss like a bird. The nuns watched as the hat spun toward the river, more slowly than quickly, halted, raised up, and then halted again by gusts of wind, sinking until it disappeared into the mist.

The praying nun prayed louder, redoubling her efforts.

Now the albino's voice darkened:

"You're going to make me lose my concentration, you cursed nuns."

XII

THE PRECIPICE SANK AWAY BENEATH THEM; THEY RESEM-
bled two tiny leaves set against that vertical landscape of stone.
Hands pressed to the wall, they continued to advance until the
midpoint of the nose. On that narrow ledge their silhouettes
stuck out against the sky, above the sky, like splinters.

"What?" said the albino. "Are we taking a breather here, exactly halfway on our journey? Go on, go on."

But he wasn't going on; and not so much due to a fear of falling, but because his strength was abandoning him. His fingers
were turning numb in the gaps between the bricks. His cheek,
his chest: he felt embraced by a sheet of ice. He would have to
change position, at least, or else his face and heart would end up
frozen. Then he turned around, carefully, painfully, and faced
the abyss, his back glued to the wall, his arms stretched out like
a crucifix, his face turned sideways.

"Ah, numbskull!" yelled the albino. "Now you want to take
charge?"

Nevertheless, he did the same thing: in spite of his sweating,
his heart was freezing too, pressed up against the bricks. He preferred to turn his back. He looked down and cried out:

"My hat, my little hat. Where is my *sombrerito*?"

He laughed again:

"If I was a child, I'd cross this in the twinkling of an eye."

He slumped back against the ice as though sitting to rest.

"Now," he said, "if only we still had that bottle, right?"

And he patted him on the shoulder:

"Go on, go on."

He was doing his damnedest to avoid looking down into the abyss, to resist that sort of magnet, the blue swirling beneath his trembling feet.

"What?" yelled the fat man. "You want to chat for a while?"

His hand grasped him by the arm.

"Go on, go on, just keep moving."

"Let go of me."

He shrugged off the hand and kept moving along. When he was nearing the edge, where the wall ended and the headland they would have to scale in order to save themselves began, he again had to stick out a leg and change position, compelled by the ice that penetrated his skin from every brick; he couldn't remember ever having felt so cold; it was as if his feet were burning from pure cold, he thought; once more, he pressed his face to the wall and received the breath of the piercing cold squarely on his back. It was the wind that had once again begun to lash against them, as if in opposition.

"Oh," said Bonifacio, "you're provoking us, little wind, you're provoking us."

For the wind swirled finely between them, twisting like a serpent between their bodies and the bricks and causing them to tremble more, penetrating them with even more cold. Then Bonifacio changed position too. Bonifacio stretched out his leg and began to turn at that moment, as the winds became narrower, sharper, like knives; his frozen hands were no longer able to grasp the junctures.

"Damn it," he said. "I think I'm going to take a little flight."

And he tried to laugh. He turned back to face the wall, but now his shoulders were no longer touching the brickwork, his hands were no use. Surprise overwhelmed and disconcerted him, and in a gesture of desperation, almost levitating, he took another step and again positioned himself with his back to the wall. Both men were now standing next to each other, almost touching:

"I need to warm my hands," the fat man whispered softly, like a secret. "It's never been so cold. Why the hell did I come out for a stroll?"

"We're almost there," he said.

"Help me."

He placed his slim but wiry arm across the albino's chest, pushing him back against the wall, as the man rubbed his hands together.

"I can't feel them," he was saying, "I can't feel a single finger."

"We're almost there."

"*Madre.*"

The wind hovered, caressing the brick ledge; they could now hear its raspy whistle climbing up to their necks, getting in through their pores. They felt every one of its gentle nudges, momentary, but nudges all the same.

"What are you playing at, Bonifacio?" came a voice.

To their right, on top of the headland, he saw the blackened figure of the cart driver against the leaden sky. And then the face of the shopkeeper appeared, his neck, his chest, his legs, his shoes, and the face of another man, a stranger.

Then, one by one, in silence, they were joined by other faces, other bodies, familiar but strange; different, he thought. The cart driver, for example, now appeared gigantic, remote, his eyes colder than the freezing bricks. And, at the same time, he noticed the first spreading shreds of mist, fragmenting the peering faces, cloaking the hands, slipping away on their breath, splitting the bodies in two.

Indifferent, standing three or four paces from the cart driver, right at the very edge, the shopkeeper continued to peer down into the abyss. It sounded as if he was laughing.

"How pigheaded," came his voice, belittling them.

"Come to us," said the cart driver now, directing his words to him alone, "come once and for all, old man, you're expected here. You've earned it."

He looked in the direction they were pointing: he made out, along the edge of the summit, among the choir of static men and women, pale in the distance—their faces like great droplets of wax—his granddaughter. She had lost at least as much weight as he had, and she was crying. He discovered that they were both crying, *she and I*, he thought, but could think no more, because the fear and vertigo were returning. On either side of his granddaughter, the women appeared, among them the dwarf, transfixed. The landlady was also looking down at him, observing his every move, as though still watching over him. And, along the far edge yellow with mist, sitting on enormous stones on the banks of the abyss, as though sprouted on the brink, he spied the children. One of them, the tallest, was now carrying the old lady's head under his arm: he held it aloft with both hands, displaying it for a moment, as if intending to explain something—or simply for a laugh—and then he threw it up into the sky, just like a soccer ball: the mist swallowed it up before the abyss. The kid continued to watch him, but he was no longer paying attention. He was once again captivated by the abyss: he thought he glimpsed the condor, flying beneath them, as if in wait. He thought he saw it for half a second, appearing and disappearing behind an instant of mist.

"Have you two still not fallen?" said the shopkeeper, craning his neck, taking yet another step at the summit. He continued to observe them, spellbound. Then, imbued with the most absolute indifference, he took off his glasses and began wiping them with the end of his scarf.

He wanted to wake from his vertigo. His granddaughter was there, he told himself. He repeated it a thousand times, as if convincing himself. Now, confused, he was able to glimpse the stranger. For the first time he could see him clearly, and this in spite of the fact that the stranger had been the person closest to him, from his position at the summit, for all this time. He wasn't sure how long the man had been pointing that rifle at them—at him and the albino, alternately.

"Should I let them have it?" he heard him ask the others.

The cart driver shook his head.

"No?" asked the stranger.

"No," said the cart driver.

The stranger hesitated for a second.

"It makes no difference," he said. And he stopped pointing the rifle and turned away from the abyss. Soon the mist began to swallow his shoulders, his back.

They were interrupted by a sound like tearing. Those leaning out over the edge turned their heads, their eyes gleaming intermittently; the sound came not from them but from behind, on the other side of the abyss: crisscrossed by shreds of mist, the terrace was a tumult of praying nuns.

No one said a thing. No one seemed to care.

Frozen, but invigorated by his anguish, he continued to explore the summit. With difficulty, he again made out the profile of his granddaughter. She was covering her eyes with her hands, still crying. He heard her muffled voice—a terrified whimper—and could barely understand her:

"Just come over here," she was saying. "They've already taken off my chains."

No one seemed to care about this either. No one said a thing.

"What?" the albino stammered, without turning to look at those peering down at him. It was as if a faraway rage still inflamed his words. "Happy to see me teetering on the edge?"

"This Bonifacio really had us all tipsy," said the shopkeeper, addressing no one in particular.

"You thought you were God Almighty," said the cart driver. "Nobody threw stones at those children, damn it."

From the top, filling the void left by the stranger, came the voice of the dwarf: she couldn't take her inflamed eyes off the albino.

"Let him get what's coming to him once and for all," she said.

The cart driver lay face down, with half his body hanging over the edge of the headland, his arm outstretched, hand at the ready:

"Come on, old man, let him go, or a righteous man will fall as a sinner."

They heard a burbling coming from the albino's chest; it was as if he were trying to say something, but no words came out, just dark water on his lips.

He could no longer hold the albino's body against the wall. He was barely able to move stiffly toward the headland and stretch out an arm. The cart driver's hand hoisted him like a log. He collapsed onto the ground, by his side. His heart ached. He wanted to embrace his granddaughter. He wanted to run away. But he turned and looked down, toward the brink of the ledge. There was the man who said he was called Bonifacio in this town. He had his eyes closed. Without a word, he tumbled into the abyss.

BOGOTÁ, 2003